FUNNY AN
Tracing Fun

by Joan Berger, Karen Braun & Anita Sperling

Illustrated by Manny Campana

ISBN 0-590-42197-2

21 20 19   6/9

34

First Scholastic printing, January 1989

SCHOLASTIC INC.
New York Toronto London Auckland Sydney

INSTRUCTIONS

Trace your own funny animal. Follow the instructions below.

1. Pick out and trace one of the face shapes on pages 4-5.

2. Trace in eyes, a nose, and ears from pages 6-8, and a mouth from page 25.

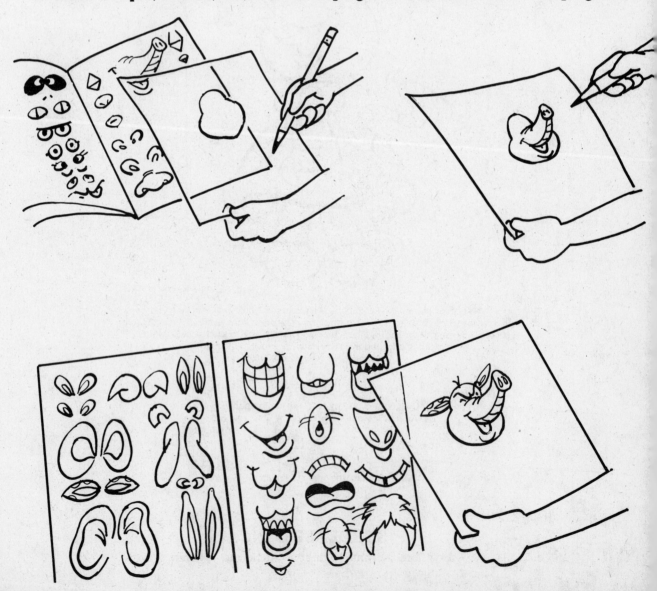

3. When your face is finished, add a body and paws from pages 26-28.

4. Trace a pair of legs from page 29.

5. Now you can add a mane, a tail, or an accessory from pages 30-32.

How many different animals can you make?

Faces

Faces

5

Eyes

Noses

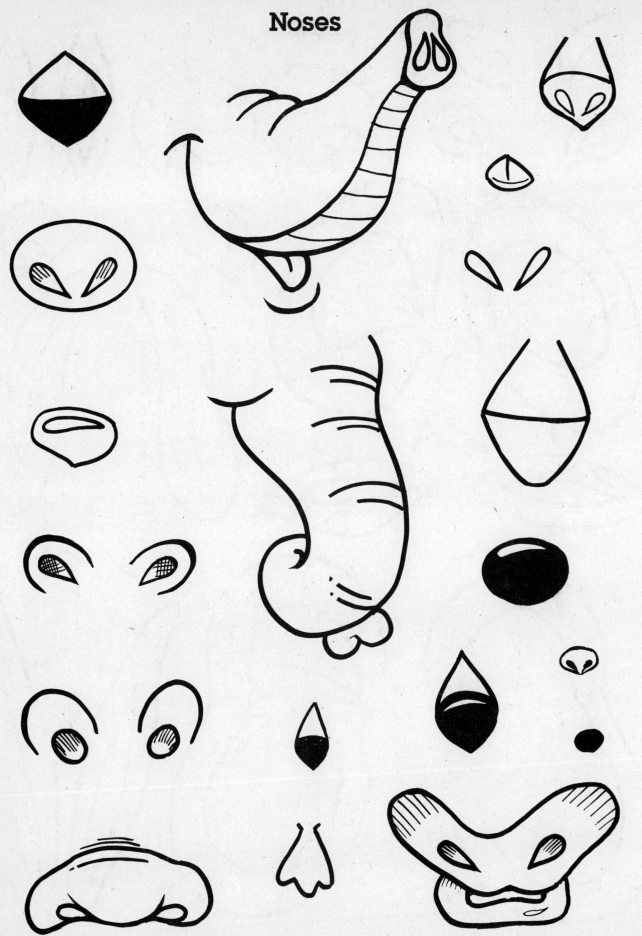

Ears

8